Santa's Christmas Prayer

CLIFF ROAD
BOOKS

Santa's Christmas Prayer

Nell Navillus

Illustrated by

Carol Newsom

CLIFF ROAD
BOOKS

It was late at night on Christmas Eve
when Santa finished delivering his sleigh full
of gifts to all the boys and girls in the world.

Santa was tired. So were the reindeer.
They hadn't eaten anything since
their early supper at the North Pole,
and it was now almost dawn.

Santa knew Mrs. Claus would be waiting at home with his favorite slippers. But he was still at least two hours away from the North Pole. There was a clearing below, near a little country church, that would make the perfect place to stop and rest.

Santa landed the sleigh in a cloud of snow. The reindeer looked gratefully at Santa as he hopped out and gathered their feed sacks, which he filled with oats.

Then Santa walked around, stretching his legs while the reindeer ate. The little church was a peaceful place on Christmas Eve, with snowbanks mounding all around, snow lacing the branches of the trees, and one candle twinkling in a window high up in the church steeple.

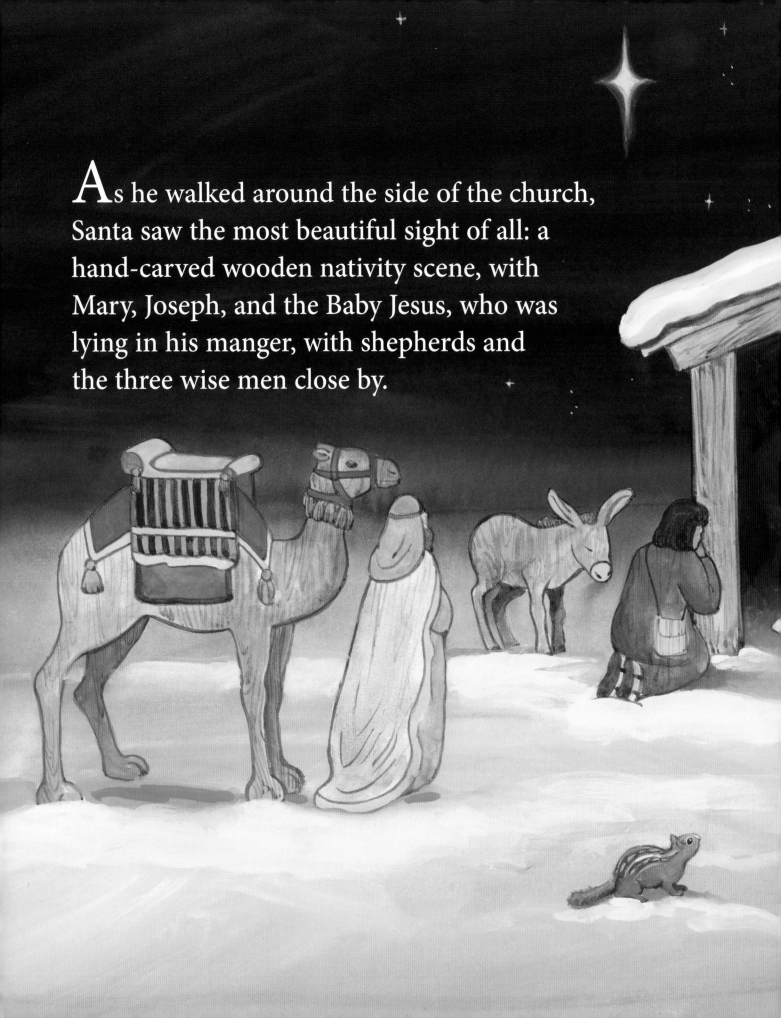

As he walked around the side of the church, Santa saw the most beautiful sight of all: a hand-carved wooden nativity scene, with Mary, Joseph, and the Baby Jesus, who was lying in his manger, with shepherds and the three wise men close by.

Someone had made this nativity with a great deal of care and love, Santa thought. The scene was so quiet and filled with peace that Santa's heart was moved. He knelt in the snow and began to pray.

"Dear Lord, to you I pray,
that the true meaning of Christmas
fill each home this day.

"I pray for boys and girls,
young and old, who may
be here with us,
or even far away,

this sacred night,

when the Son of G   u

For nothing can match the wonder and love
that Jesus brought when he came from above.

"He gave true love and eternal life,
the gifts most precious in our sight.

"I am humbly thankful for the role I play
in making children happy on Christmas Day.

"But dear Lord, let us all keep in mind
it is you who gives the gift of our lives."

Santa returned to his sleigh, and the reindeer lifted off into the night. Far below, the preacher's son came to ring the church bell at dawn ... and was just in time to hear a jolly voice calling, "God bless us everyone!"